HANSY'S MERMAID

Trinka Hakes Noble

The Dial Press 🦁 *New York*

JP

Published by
The Dial Press
1 Dag Hammarskjold Plaza
New York, New York 10017

Design by Susan Lu
First printing

Library of Congress Cataloging in Publication Data
Noble, Trinka Hakes. Hansy's mermaid.
Summary: A storm brings a mermaid to a Dutch family
that puts her to work for them; but the young son, Hansy,
longs to help her return to her home in the sea.
[1.Mermaids—Fiction.   2.Netherlands—Fiction]
I. Title.
PZ7.N6715Han 1983   [E]   82-45509
ISBN 0-8037-3605-3
ISBN 0-8037-3606-1 (lib. bdg.)

The art for each picture consists of a pencil and wash
drawing with three pencil overlays reproduced
in black, yellow, red, and blue halftone.

For A.M.N.
May your sails be forever filled with wind.

One spring long ago a fierce storm began to blow across the Zuider Zee. The windmills stood tall and brave, guarding the low green land, but the storm was much too powerful. The surging waters broke through the dikes and swept past the windmills. They surrounded the little Dutch farmhouses and sent the cows running helter-skelter across the flat meadows of North Holland.

After the storm had passed and the dikes were repaired, Farmer Klumperty and his good wife called their four children.

"Now, my good ladykins," said Papa Klumperty to the three stout daughters, "go to the far meadow and look for our cows. They will need fresh water after the storm."

"And, Hansy," said Mama Klumperty to their little son, "bring your cart quickly. I want you to take our butter and cheese to the canal boat. It will be sailing to market soon."

Hansy filled his cart and started down the canal road.

Clara, Freenia, and Purleenia filled their buckets and danced off through the wet fields to find the cows.

When they reached the far meadow, Clara suddenly saw something flashing in the sunlight.

"What's that?" she cried.

The three quickly gathered around a pool where a shiny silver-blue tail was jerking and twisting in the water.

"Why, it's a fish swept in by the storm," said Freenia.

"It will make a fine dinner," said Purleenia.

But as she reached for the fish she suddenly jumped back.

"It's not a fish," she screamed. "It's a mermaid!"

The three sisters watched in disbelief as a beautiful girl with the tail of a fish and hair the color of seaweed struggled in the pool before them.

"How strange," said Clara. "Let's take her home."

The trapped mermaid fought with all her might to escape. She wanted only to return to the sea. Everything she loved was there—the salt water, the waves, her home and friends—everything! But the three sisters were too strong for her and they carried her off to Klumperty Farm.

Papa ran from the barn, Mama and Hansy hurried from the creamery, and Granny Klumperty came hobbling up the brick path to see this strange thing washed in by the flood.

"What are we going to do with her?" asked Hansy as he fed the mermaid and gently tried to calm her down.

Granny Klumperty shook her head. "We have no place for a mermaid on Klumperty Farm."

"Aye," agreed Mama. "She must be taught to work so she can earn her keep."

"But why don't we put her back in the sea?" asked Hansy.

"Nay, Hansy," said Papa sternly. "In the sea she would only be another mermaid. But here she can learn to be useful and better herself. Just wait, soon she will thank us for it."

"But," objected Hansy, "wouldn't she be happier living in the water as a mermaid? Why must she be like us?"

"You silly boy," scolded Clara. "Don't you know that to be like us is the best you can be?"

And so everyone except Hansy agreed they would teach the mermaid to be a proper farm girl.

First they let down the hem of a homespun dress so as to hide the mermaid's long tail. Then they tied a durable apron around her middle. Only Hansy thought to ask the mermaid her name.

"Seanora," she answered.

"Hansy!" Clara said sharply. "There's no time for chitchat. We must do something with this ridiculous hair." And she tucked the mermaid's long sea-green hair under a snug white cap.

In the weeks that followed, Hansy had no chance to talk to Seanora. Everyone was so busy teaching her to be useful. Clara and Freenia taught her to churn the cheese and pat the butter. Granny Klumperty taught her to sew and to spin. Purleenia taught her to tat the lace for caps and collars.

And when the mermaid was not busy at all this, Mama taught her to scrub and scour everything—dishes, pots, pans, windows, walls, floors, front steps, brick paths, and even the family's wooden shoes. In no time the mermaid was quite made over. All that spring she sewed and spun, she churned and patted and tatted, she scrubbed and scoured.

Then they congratulated themselves.

"We have done fine work," they said. "Why, she's almost as good as we are!"

Only Hansy noticed the sadness in the mermaid's eyes. Often he would come and sit before her, watching her.

"Dear Seanora," he asked her one day, "why are you so sad?"

"Oh, Hansy, I fear I shall not last long," answered the mermaid softly. "I need the water. I need to play with waves…to dive with dolphins…to soar with the flying fish…."

"I would carry you to the canal this very instant," declared Hansy bravely, "if…if only I knew which one leads to the sea. There are so many canals, and they are so very long. If you swam in the wrong direction, you would get lost…or caught by a fisherman's hook!"

Seanora gasped.

"Maybe you will grow to like it here," said Hansy gently.

But as the days went by, the mermaid grew only sadder and sadder. Hansy became worried. "I must find a way to cheer her up," he thought.

One day while Hansy was delivering the butter and cheese to the canal boat, he noticed a strong salty smell. Looking down, he saw a clump of seaweed stuck to the bottom of the boat. "Hmm...I wonder," thought Hansy. He waded into the water and quickly snatched the seaweed. He wrapped it in a cheesecloth and hurried home.

He waited until his sisters were too busy to notice, and then he presented the mermaid with his gift from the sea.

As she opened the cheesecloth a fresh salty smell of the open sea arose and a lovely bloom appeared upon her face.

"Oh, Hansy," Seanora cried. "Seaweed salad! My favorite!"

All that afternoon, as Seanora nibbled on the tangy seaweed, she told Hansy about her seashell collection and her little house set among tall seaweed. She told him how she would play water tag with the mermen and mermaids and how they would sun themselves on the rocks. Oh, how the mermaid wished to live in the sea where nothing needed scrubbing, where sewing was unheard of, and no one ate butter and cheese!

And so the summer days went by. Hansy brought seaweed salad as often as he could. Many times Seanora would help him sail his paper boats, and then she would tell him tales of her life at sea.

When the cold weather came to north Holland, the cows gave less milk, and so there was less butter and cheese to make. It was holiday time for the Dutch children. The canals froze and everyone went ice-skating. Even Clara, Freenia, and Purleenia stopped working and got down their skates.

At this Seanora became puzzled.

"But surely you will get wet," she said.

"No, silly," said Clara. "The water turns to ice."

"Ice?" asked the mermaid. "What is ice?"

The three sisters laughed.

"You'll never find out," they said. "We don't have any skates that fit fish tails!"

"Never mind," said Hansy. "I have fixed it so she won't need ice skates."

Hansy had removed the wheels from his cart and fastened on wooden runners.

"This will make a perfect sleigh for you," he said as he tucked a woolen blanket around Seanora's long tail.

How the mermaid loved gliding over the ice with Hansy! For the very first time she tilted back her head and laughed.

Hansy thought it was the most beautiful sound he had ever heard and he wished winter would never end.

But all too soon March came—that stormy month when winter makes its last stand. When Hansy arrived at the canal boat, the wind was blowing hard from the north.

"Hansy, my lad," shouted the captain, "best hurry home. A storm's coming!"

"A mighty storm?" asked Hansy.

"Aye, lad, the Zuider Zee is rising. We fear that the dikes are cracking. Hurry along home or you'll be swept out to sea."

Hansy began to run. The wind seemed to be screaming "Sea-nor-a," and the clattering wheels of his cart seemed to chant "Swept-out-to-sea, swept-out-to-sea." The tower bells began to sound a wild alarm, but all Hansy could hear was "Sea-nor-a, swept-out-to-sea, Sea-nor-a…"

There was so much excitement at home that no one noticed when he and Seanora disappeared into the growing darkness.

"I'm taking you to the far meadow," shouted Hansy. "It will surely flood."

The mermaid sat upright, her nose twitching at the strong salt smell.

Hansy took the mermaid to the middle of the low pasture and lifted her from the cart.

"You must follow the tides out to sea, Seanora," he warned, "and you must be careful and you must swim strongly and you must—"

"Don't worry, Hansy," said Seanora. "I know everything about the sea."

"Oh, of course…I forgot…." said Hansy.

And then from the direction of the sea came a sound that slowly grew and swelled to a roar.

"Hansy! FLEE! Quickly—to high ground!"

Hansy scrambled up the canal bank to safety. Then he turned and saw only dark waters where the mermaid had been.

"Good-bye, beautiful Seanora. I'll miss you!" he cried.

And very faintly from far away he heard "I shall never forget you, Hansy! Never!"

When the storm had passed and the dikes were repaired, Clara,
Freenia, and Purleenia carried fresh water to the cows in the far
pasture. They returned carrying the mermaid's wet and muddy cap,
apron, and dress.

"She must have gone back to the sea," they exclaimed.

"Oh, well, her lace wasn't as fine as mine," said Purleenia.

"Aye, and her butter was too salty!" shrugged Freenia.

"And her cheese tasted fishy!" snipped Clara.

"She never could have been as good as we are," they agreed.

"That's true." Hansy laughed. "She'd never be like you!"

Years went by, and Clara, Freenia, and Purleenia grew up to be the best butter and cheese makers in all of north Holland. Hansy grew up to be a fine sea captain. His ship carried his sisters' famous butter and cheese all over the world. And although Hansy sailed the seas far and wide, the fiercest storm never blew his ship off course, and he always returned safely to port.

Many believe that the mermaid of north Holland never forgot Hansy. Never!

jP

Noble
    Hansy's mermaid.
                            68604
                            (10.95)

9/89